To ....

For being good.
MERRY
CHRISTMAS!
From Santa

To my family ... the best present ever x

Visit the author's website! http://ericjames.co.uk

Written by Eric James
Illustrated by Robert Dunn and Katherine Kirkland
Designed by Sarah Allen

Published by Sourcebooks Jabberwocky, an imprint of Sourcebooks, Inc.
P.O. Box 4410, Naperville, Illinois 60567-4410
(630) 961-3900
Fax: (630) 961-2168
jabberwockykids.com

Date of Production: June 2017
Run Number: HTW_PO100417
Printed and bound in China (GD)
10 9 8 7 6 5 4 3 2

Santa's Sleigh
is on its way to
Canada

sourcebooks
jabberwocky

The moon over Canada casts a cool glow.
Ottawa lies snug under blankets of snow.
The star-sprinkled sky is especially bright.

"Hey Santa! Hey Santa!
Please visit tonight!"

The snowmen in Surrey stand perfectly still,
Their hats and their scarves keeping out the night chill.

The icicles sparkle as snowflakes drift down
From **Faro** to **Charlottetown,** and all around.

The Christmas trees twinkle,
The eggnog smells sweet,
The stockings are out
(for the gifts, not your feet!)

The garlands and
paper-chains
hang from
the ceiling,
And give the
whole household
that Christmassy
feeling.

They scurry upstairs,
for they've heard
it is said
That Santa comes
once you're asleep
in your bed!

Excited young children
with heads full of wishes
Leave large Christmas cookies
and carrots on dishes.

The yawns in Toronto grow stronger and stronger.
The children of Brandon can't stay up much longer.
From Springfield to Sydney and Montreal too,
They're soon sleeping soundly,

All children but you!

Happy Xmas

SANTA
STOP
HERE!

You stand at your window
and gaze at the sky,
With hopes that you'll see
Santa's sleigh *whizzing* by.
You almost nod off,
but see movement ahead...

...A flurry of white and some flashes of red!

You jump up and down as the shape becomes clear.
"Hey Santa! Hey Santa!
My home's over here!"

But something is wrong. There are sparks EVERYWHERE.
The sleigh *twists* and *turns* as it swoops through the air.

You're wide awake now.
You've had such a fright.
There's no chance of sleep
till you know he's alright.

You think about Santa,
his reindeer and sleigh.
"Hey Santa!
Hey Santa!
I hope you're okay!"

Yes, Santa is fine!
He is in **Stanley Park**,
Replacing the fuse for his sleigh (in the dark).

He tugs on the reins, shouting,
"UP, UP, AWAY!"
And hits the ignition,
which starts up his sleigh.

STANLEY
PARK

With magical speed only Santa possesses, he visits well over a thousand addresses.

From Oakville to Edmonton
handing out toys,
He visits each house
without making a noise.

Now Santa has been to all houses but one.
He can't go back home till this last house is done.

It's YOUR house, of course, but you're still wide awake.
He circles above as he takes a small break.
And that's when you see him. You know he's alright!
Your head hits the pillow. You're out like a light.

He lands on the roof to the sound of your snores.
"It's Santa! It's Santa!
He's coming indoors!"

But, ARGH!

You wake up and you jump to your feet.

You're sure you forgot to leave Santa a treat.

Will Santa leave presents for someone so rude?!

You must go downstairs

and make sure he has food!

You enter the kitchen
and turn on the light,
Not spotting the figure
who ducks out of sight.

You're still half-asleep,
so you don't find it weird
That the broom has a hat

...and a coat
...and a beard!

You get out the cookies, still rubbing your eyes,
Too blurry to make out his clever disguise.
You open the fridge door,

but don't spot the **broom**

As it sweeps past you into...

...the family room!

With a plate in your hands, you head off to the tree.
You're feeling so sleepy you don't even see
A sight that would have your heart
skipping a beat—
The curtains have sprouted...

...two Santa-sized feet!

Still sleepy, you head back
to bed with a smile.
The panic is over.
It's all been worthwhile.

You climb up the staircase,
not once looking back,
As a chuckling Santa
takes toys from his sack.

Ho,
ho,
ho

Now Santa is leaving. His sleigh races high.
It sparkles and fizzles and lights up the sky.

The Vancouver streetlights
grow dim in the night.

"Hey Santa! Hey Santa!
Please have a safe flight!"

Soon Santa leaves Canada's cities behind,
Where children are lovely, and grown-ups are kind.
And then he booms loudly,
his voice full of cheer...

"Ho, ho, ho! Canada, I'll see you next year!"

The Twins Go to Iceland

VOLUME 2
THE TWINS GO SERIES

*This book is dedicated to my beautiful twins.
I hope you remember the fun you had in Iceland!*

Olivia and Jack are excited
to greet a brand new day.

They're traveling in Iceland,
and they can't wait to play.

Iceland is a country that
gets very, very cold.

The capital is Reykjavik,
which is beautiful and old.

The people in Iceland say words
that are really, really long,

6

and their ancestors were Vikings, who were very big and strong.

Iceland has sheep, glaciers, mountains, and ice.

It even has a spot where
two continents collide.

In Iceland,
you can see
puffins and the
amazing Northern
lights, which paint colors
across the sky and
brighten up the night.

Iceland also has hot springs
and magnificent pools.

Take a shower before jumping in
because that's their rule!

The best hot spring in Iceland
is called the Blue Lagoon,

and the twins' parents let them
swim there all afternoon.

When you meet an Icelander,
ask them about elves and trolls,

and take a boat to see the whales,
which are a sight to behold.

Overall, the twins enjoyed their trip
and seeing a brand new place,
learning long Icelandic words,
and finding a new culture to embrace.

It's always fun for them
to go to a new country.
They can't wait for their next adventure.
Who knows where that will be?

THE
END

19

About the Author

Catherine Alford wrote her first children's book when she was a little girl. It was called "The Talking Road," and it was about a child who got lost, but luckily, found a talking road that helped her find her way home. Nearly 20 years later, Catherine is a full time writer and CEO of a boutique media company that provides written and video content to companies all across the world.

She is happily married to her husband, and together they have boy/girl twins who were born in March 2014.

This book series is inspired by them, with a goal to help them and kids everywhere develop a love of travel and an interest in other cultures.

www.catherinealford.com

Jaime Espinar's love of art comes from his family heritage. He is the son, grandson, and brother of artists. He studied Fine Arts in college and has extensive experience creating art in a variety of mediums from paintings to scenery for theatre and television. He has been creating custom illustrations since 2005, working in advertising, magazines, Internet media, and publishing.

Currently, he's focused on creating children's book illustrations, comics, and even game design. He has illustrated over 50 children's books thus far, and he thoroughly enjoys collaborating with authors to bring their work to life. Jaime currently resides in Spain with his wife, who is a graphic designer, and their two cats.

jaimeespinar.wordpress.com

LEARN MORE ABOUT THE TWINS GO SERIES

CONNECT WITH US ONLINE:

Website: www.TheTwinsGo.com

Twitter: @TheTwinsGo
Facebook: www.facebook.com/TheTwinsGo
Instagram: TheTwinsGo
Hashtag: Use #TheTwinsGo to show us your travels or your favorite book!

E-mail: Cat@CatherineAlford.com

The Twins Go book series is published by:

The *Alford* Media Group

❋ *a boutique media company* ❋

For more information about the author, please visit:

www.catherinealford.com

The Blue Lagoon in Iceland - 2016

Our books are inspired by our real life
family adventures. We hope you enjoy them.
Love,
The Alfords

Made in the USA
Middletown, DE
30 July 2018